For Oscar and Erik,
Who love their food

First published in 2018 by Scholastic Children's Books
Euston House, 24 Eversholt Street, London NW1 1DB
a division of Scholastic Ltd
www.scholastic.co.uk
London ~ New York ~ Toronto ~ Sydney ~ Auckland ~ Mexico City ~ New Delhi ~ Hong Kong

Text and illustrations copyright © 2018 Jo Williamson

ISBN 978 1407 16214 0

10 9 8 7 6 5 4 3 2 1

The moral rights of Jo Williamson have been asserted.
Papers used by Scholastic Children's Books are made
from wood grown in sustainable forests.

WHAT'S FOR LUNCH, PAPA PENGUIN?

Jo Williamson

SCHOLASTIC

Papa Penguin and Pippin ran the **best** café in the Antarctic. They served fish.

Fish for breakfast . . . Fish for lunch . . . Fish for dinner!

Fried fish . . .   baked fish . . .

grilled fish . . .

boiled fish.

Even fish
ice cream!

Everyone
loved fish.

Yum!

TODAY

FRIED FISH
FISHY LOLLIES
FISH PANCAKES

Or *did* they?
One day, Frank
suddenly blurted out,

"I'm fed up with fish!
I want something
different!"

Papa Penguin
didn't know
what to do.

Hmm

He thought hard . . .

Err

Ummm

Aha!

until . . .

. . . he had an **idea!**

Back soon!

The journey seemed to take . . .

. . . a very long time.

But finally . . .

...they were THERE!

"Now let's look for NEW food," said Papa Penguin.

"But nobody eats **sticks**," chuckled Pippin.

"WE do!" said the pandas.

"Bamboo is . . .
err . . . delicious,"
smiled Papa Penguin,
politely.

"And very BENDY!"
laughed Pippin.

Next, the map led them to a land of hot hills.
"This looks interesting," pondered Papa Penguin.
"But please stay still until I find out where we are."

"*I'm* not moving," said Pippin.
"But . . .

When they stopped, the kind
camels gave Papa Penguin
and Pippin some nuts, seeds
and delicious dates
for their trolley.

As Papa Penguin and Pippin travelled further,
they discovered even more exciting foods.

Bread and rolls . . .

cheese with holes . . .

bakes and cakes ...

chocolate shakes!

Along their journey, they even found a place selling
fabulous fruit of all colours, shapes and sizes.
And Pippin was a great help . . .

. . . most of the time.

Grrrrrr
Grrrrrr!

Eventually, it was time
to head home!

"We DID it!" cried Papa Penguin.

"And I was NO trouble!" added Pippin.

They couldn't wait to start cooking.

The penguin pair got to work.
They baked and basted ...

tested and tasted ...

sliced ...
  diced ...
    and iced ...

until finally, the
café was ready
to open.

The new-look café was bursting with customers, all eager to try the fantastic new food.

"What would YOU like, Frank?" asked Papa Penguin proudly.

There was so much choice that Frank found it hard to decide.

But finally, he replied . . .

"Just FISH, please!"